Beautifully Faded

Compiled By
Prachita Arora
Risha Jagga

Published by InkQuills Publishing House
www.inkquills.in

First Edition 2020
All Rights Reserved. Copyright © 2020

ISBN: 978-81-945636-4-8

DISCLAIMER

The published write-ups are the original contents of the co-authors and compiler had done its best to edit and make it plagiarism free.

The characters may be fictitious or based on real events but they are not meant to hurt anyone's feeling nor portray anything against any caste or system.

In case of any plagiarized write-up the co-author is solely responsible for it, Compiler or Publisher would not be responsible for it.

Prachita Arora

Risha Jagga

ACKNOWLEDGEMENT

To write a good poetry is what a writer dreams of and to get it published is a cherry on the cake. Beautifully Faded is a short poetry anthology compiled by Prachita Arora and Risha Jagga.

This anthology wouldn't have been possible without the active involvement of our co-authors who were supportive and made our book more beautiful. It was all because of your hard work and excitement towards this beautiful project.

Kudos to you all.

Also we would like to thank our parents for believing in us and also InkQuills Publishing House for trusting us and giving this beautiful opportunity.

WAHEGURUJI MEHAR KARI!!!

COMPILER

Prachita Arora, is 20 years old and belongs to Haryana. She is currently pursuing her bachelor's degree and aims to become a fashion designer and a successful author. She is making efforts in finding out more opportunities and resources to get the best out of her.

Her creative mind helps her think widely and out of the box. She started writing to express herself and now has come so far that she is a co-author for more than thirty anthologies and has also compiled more than ten anthologies. She loves writing about realistic topics.

Her hobbies include dancing, cooking, DIY, coloring and designing. In simple words, she is a girl that believes in creativity and art. She puts happiness and satisfaction at first and writing gives her both. Her journey has been quite challenging but she is satisfied to find herself on the right platform.

To reach her, you can contact on her personal Instagram handle @poetic_shadow and for reading write-ups checkout @my_mini_tales.

SELF LOVE IS ALL WHAT YOU NEED

"When life throws you at the bed of thrones,

Self-love is the first thing that's needed to be worn;

You don't need to think what others gonna say,

Because they will not make your way,

Don't forget to, motivate yourself each day,

And when you feel low just go under the sky and lay;

Watch the beautiful moon and star,

Feel them as they are not so far;

Just like them you need to shine,

For that magic in you is what you need to find,

Don't worry, in time, everything will be fine.

And when you feel like quitting,

Just high up your pitch and shout,

"I am gonna shine, everything will be fine,

Because I have found the

Magic in Me,

I may have lost the battle but I have found Me,

And I believe Me is better than We."

COMPILER

Risha Jagga, D/O Mr. OM PRAKASH JAGGA.

Silence lover but a rising voice, she is full of grace. She's often caught with a cup of tea and notepad in the pocket. Moulding emotions and feelings of others by deep observation is her hobby.

Girl with a beautiful soul, smile, and statements make her write some good thoughts, Stories, and Poetries.

Risha is co-author in more than 50 anthologies and is part of Vajra World Record, twice. And has compiled 5 anthologies till now, you can read her thoughts on YourQuote and Instagram @diary_of_love_pain_

<u>I CHANGED</u>

Reading some old quotes
Laughing on. Some of the notes
Stories of love
Some imaginations and some realizations
Some real conversations and some dreams
And everything vanished like those good habits vanished
from my veins...

Habit of healing everyone's pain
Habit of being available every time
Habit of! Habit of being habitual of you
You! You my dear heart, your feelings sucks, it always gets
stuck
And throws me inside a memories truck
Where I am with everyone but reality is only me.
Only me! "Writing this quote" for reading it.
Reading it in future for making my soul smile
Smile again on my silly mistakes.

Here I am changing my habits again
From being mingle to single, I am removing the tag from
my head "from forever alone to a girl who owns everyone's
heart".

No! No I am not entering into a relationship
I am transferring my heart from a quarantine zone to a
garden full of butterflies.

Reading some old quotes
Laughing on some of the notes
I realized that I am changed allot

So, I am changing again and putting the note in my wallet,
I will read it the same day of next year, just to calculate the
flow of journey.

From reading to writing
From writing to loosing
From losing to realizing
Form realizing to lose
Lost to getting up
From getting up to writing
From writing to Reading again

My life is a mess and I love being a mess, because only that
time I see my perfection

Oops! I am again lost in reading and writing...

Smile please! Not for the one who is looking at you, but
for the one you always notice in the mirror.

CO-AUTHORS

Beautifully Faded

Aafreen Zafar

(IG: @_the_tiny_taless)

<u>STRONG</u>

I know you're broken, love;

I know you're in pain

I know it hurts

Every time you pick a piece of yourself

It pricks,

I know it's hard

I know.

But hang in there

You're going to get through this,

You're going to fix yourself,

You're going to be strong again,

You're going to live again,

You're going to love again,

But until then,

Stay strong love,

Stay strong.

<u>SUNSHINE</u>

I know all you see now are dark clouds, closing up on you -
making you feel like you'll never feel the light shine upon you
again - like you'll never feel the warmth of the sun against you
again.
But trust me,
It's all going to be okay.
You are going to be okay
The sun will shine upon you.
It will pave a way,
Against all those dark clouds that surround you and shine on
you.
It will happen.
The warmth of the sun will touch your skin.
The light of the sun will shine upon you.
You will feel alive again
You will feel free again
You will live
You will laugh
And yes
You will love again
Just hang in there
It's all going to be okay
Because remember – "A flower cannot blossom without
sunshine, and man cannot live without love."

Beautifully Faded

Aayushi Singh

(IG: @ayush.hi93)

<u>AS EVERYONE LEFT HER</u>

As everyone left her

Like a winter tree

Even the birds which were

Once her companion

Were ready to migrate...

And she was there

Alone

In harsh, freezing

Dreary winter

Her leaves were falling

And were demonstration

Of her looming pleas

She reminisces

Her ever-emerald beauty

Heated tears came out from

Her hollow dry eyes

Though she was

Going to be all-alone

She was more grown up

Beautifully Faded

And was used to sacrifices

"Are you crying?" they asked

"These are dew drops dear"

After enchanting these lines

She was Left

All alone

In Specter-Grey Winter.

Abi

(IG: @priyadharahini1811)

<u>FADED BY HER SOUL</u>

How to describe your resplendency,

You are a blissful song,

You are an angel,

You are an elegant painting,

You are a magnificent flower,

Your comeliness just optically incapacitates me,

You are different from other ladies,

Your comeliness stands with your vigor,

Yes, maybe you are acid attack victim,

So, you are resplendent the way you are,

You are enlightened my soul and life by your wonderfulness.

Adarsh Hegde

(IG: @wall_me_key)

BURNING DESIRE UNDER COTTON SHIRT

Your beauty sizzles, can burn thousand roses

Don't pour that much love, don't know If I could handle overdoses.

Your eyes teasing me, I thought they were shy

I say my heart's beating normal; it would be a pure lie.

Mere seconds with you feels never ending, now I've spent the whole night.

My words had lost sparks, now they have hundred poems to write.

Adewoyin Babajide John

(IG: @eight_infinity)

<u>SONDER</u>

I have come to the realization that

Each passer-by has a life as vivid and complex as mine.

Some find joy and peace of mind under the rain,

Others, the colors of the sky beyond the setting sun;

The light that shines when we feel the overwhelming urge to give up.

While some gaze into the distance without a thought,

Others trigger emotional responses too deep and mysterious for words;

The fear that time is running out to achieve life's goals -- literally gate shutting panic,

And some never cease to find something good without even looking for it—Serendipity

Beautifully Faded

<u>PEOPLE DON'T VALUE</u>

People do not value
Scars anymore--
Birth marks, stretch marks
Or scars from childhood.

It disgusts them
To embrace their wounds
Or brokenness.
Hence, they see it
As imperfection that
Should be impermanent.
That they are flaws
and should be hidden
from inspection.

So they conceal with dresses,
White dusts and makes ups...
Or even surgeries.

For they are not aware
That the pristine is less beautiful
Than the broken,
That the shape of us
Is impossible to see
Until it is fractured
And that we can only
Make things beautiful
From the scars we have had
when we are not perfect.

Adiba Imam

(IG: @_the_girl_from_saturn)

<u>IT'S OKAY</u>

It's okay all you did today is survive

At least you didn't give up

It's okay to make mistakes

Give all your harness bell a shake

Dear at least you're not fake.

It's okay to not figured out yet,

keep trying,

At least you are still on

It's okay to be lost

Dear, you've already been tossed

Hope for the head, finger crossed

Don't take your steps back, forget the loss.

Go high up in the mountains, sing your favourite song

Dear, you are strong, you're strong, you're strong.

It's okay you just forgot who you are

WELCOME BACK!

Beautifully Faded

<u>SHE</u>

Her life is smiling at her,

TO what shall I compare her,

"That is as fair as she."

Her troubles are ashamed

Because she never complained,

Of that strange sense, its silence framed.

Her tears are frozen,

'Oh God she is still not broken'

For the countless confused, accused, misused, strung-out
ones and worse.

They all failed...

Who says she is a curse,

She is alone the damn universe.

Beautifully Faded

Aditya Mande

(IG: @caffeinated_adi)

<u>TO YOUR BEST FRIEND</u>

A sweet friendship embraces the soul

A genuine friendship is always cherished

A beautiful friendship inspires the self

A trustworthy friendship never leaves.

This friendship is candor

A friendship which stays

A friendship which is an epitome

An epitome which defines you.

I love your fun filled personality

Which somehow never fails to impress

I cherish your words of love

Which awe me with its grace

I know our pages of friendship will

grow along the path and glow

The twists and turns may come along

But they will channelize our flow

Beautifully Faded

You are dearest to me
My definition of splendor
The one who paints my life
With her own colors of luster.

I am blessed to have you
And will not let you go what may
For I know that you are someone
Who is here to stay.

Adyasha

(IG: @_itz_.k._adyasha_)

LOST CHILDHOOD

No fear from dark sunshine.

Crazy is the childhood memories of mine.

Father's hand holding my hand,

My plays with the sand.

Mud making my dresses dirty,

Mom's love with the word ' naughty'

My world was surrounded by toys.

When no one was there to limit my joy

Birthdays rocked with all,

Me the exception, as all were tall

Mistakes with small heights were acceptable.

Now no one cares by thinking me capable.

I can't go back to my past.

But pictures were clicked to have a repeat telecast.

<u>THE MESMERIZED SOUL</u>

My eyes are open to see the reality,

Where I belong to a false city.

Some people around me are with dirty minds,

And good people are whom I need to find.

Their faces are covered with a sense of selfishness,

I had tolerated as my heart was full of kindness.

My head is covered with questions and answers to be found,

But I was unable to detect even the cheating sound.

My ideas about double faced people are like touching stars in the sky,

My only wish from God is to hear my cry.

When people needed me helping them was my fault,

And when they don't then I realized my insult.

But now it's enough to tolerate their bad deeds.

It's time to return their deeds by fulfilling my early needs.

Beautifully Faded

Arika Rohal

(IG: @rohal___)

<u>REST IN PEACE ~ PSYCHO</u>

Whatever she had,

She was elated,

Don't know why everyone hated?

"Everyone has problems in life"so do I,

'You live in imaginary world' this fact she deny.

Her words do not match with actions,

INSANE, CRAZY, PSYCHO she was called ,

And in dire need of injections.

Doctors find out her mentally unstable,

Listening to this she babble.

"My parents passed away,

My husband left me,

Their spirits are here, I can see".

A healthy person just faded,

Passed away before she could be aided.

<u>MY MOM</u>

A girl married at eighteen,

Since then here she has been.

She too had a dream,

No one bothered she scream.

Dominated by relatives,

But her best she gives.

Sacrificed her life,

Becoming good daughter, mother and wife.

Respect she has now earned,

But what about the dreams she burned.

What she is and what she could be,

I am her daughter her future in me she can see.

Giving birth to a girl was not your fault ,

But you protected me from assault.

Beautifully Faded

Alipsha Mallick

(IG: @alipshamallickk)

AWAKENING THOUGHT AT MIDNIGHT

It's late summer midnight,

And there is darkness and silence ruling over the realm.

The world is probably sleeping,

I can see people in my head,

On their bed,

Resting in skydivers position.

They are perhaps consumed by their summer dreams,

Of sunbathing at the Californian beach,

And young men playing water polo amidst the blues.

And here I am,

The only wonderer still awake, I guess,

Who is suffering from insomnia and anxiety disorders!

It's a cold night in my bed,

And my body is embroidered skillfully to my blanket.

There are my fingers under the sheet,

That run like lighting

On the brilliant screen of my dearest pal.

(Probably my only pal)

At this hour, when everyone's sweat-drenched body lean to
their cozy mattresses,

Beautifully Faded

Mine is apparently getting chills by the unconscious feelings,

Soaring and tumbling in the space of my mind.

Beautifully Faded

Alka Vyas

(IG: @__avwrites)

<u>HIS PRESENCE</u>

When everyday she kissed him...

When everyday she cooked for him...

When night and day were held in her palms...

When moon was bright as sun in her arms...

When he looked at her beyond her flaws...

When he kissed and made her world pause...

When every night was filled with passion...

When he made love to her in old fashion...

They smiled together throughout their lives...

Till the day his last breath said good bye...

She had no choice but to move on...

But she had his last voice to cling on...

In bed when she went...

Put her thoughts to rewind

With his face and smell clouding her mind

She waited for his arms to engulf her round

Instead she was left with just his sound

"Hey babe m running a little late...

But I will come soon in the world we create

Beautifully Faded

I will let your scent in my system flow...

And sleep in your arms, till the world ends, that you know!

See u soon my baby's mother

I will be home in an hour another"

And with that she would start snoring lightly...

With closed moist eyes and his picture... hugged tightly!

Amita Prabhakar

(IG : @amita_prabhakar)

<u>LONELINESS</u>

Loneliness is not bad always...

Sometimes it tells us "who am I? "

It made me realize that "I am the boss of my life and control of my life is in my hands ".

Loneliness is not bad always...

Loneliness gives reality check to our inner capability in a form of creativity. It is a best time to improve our creativity.

Loneliness is not bad always...

Loneliness repairs your heart by giving solution of your problem and gives the power to fight against problems.

Loneliness is not bad always...

Make loneliness is the strength of your life and enjoy it because it is a best time to understand the self. Live the life in the way you love when you are alone.

Loneliness is not bad always...

Anasua Basu

(IG: @a_n_a_s_u_a)

<u>MIDNIGHT MEETING</u>

Again, Today I am going to meet my DADDY at night…

He has amended himself a lot in these years…

Some weird exhibitions caught my mind…

His cheerful countenance has got hollowed with unkempt
torments…

He still has the chiseled nose cut down from a rose…

But fingers are no more standing in their backbone…certainly,
wretched…

His stances carried away the unnoticed dentures which have
no teeth at all!!!!??

Hahaha!!! but only spoilt gums…

His torso looked like a chain of mountains crumbling, and
getting splattered by windfall… He wears a nightmare with a
cloak on its base… He debased zig-zag; he exclaimed those
are zany kind!!!

He still narrated me those anecdotes of fairies… till my mom
calls…He gets soluble with dust and withered leaves… Bid me
a good morning for today's night… I put his belongings
along with his desires… let me tell you I am in a necropolis,
but the other spirits haunting me, coming from their nests…
I cannot conceal anymore… become a kinship of them…
come and join these spirits… Yes!!! We are together again.

Beautifully Faded

Anjali Chhajer

(IG: @poetry_dilettante)

<u>I WANT TO LIVE</u>

I want to live in a world where nobody questions my words,

I want to live in a world where I can freely fly like a bird,

I want to live in a world where people love me for what and who I am, not for what they want me to be.

I want to live in a world where I set my targets, my goals and follow my dreams passionately, not on what people decide for me.

I want to live in a world where no one is black or white, no one is rich or poor where no one is employer or employee, no one is boss or servant, I want to live in a world where everyone is treated equally.

But…

I don't want to live in a world where people say something else and mean something else.

I don't want to live in a world where people wear a mask, where people wear a mask of fake smile, wear a mask of fake concern, wear a fake mask that they're with you through thick and thin but in reality they don't even care about you.

I am a simple person, I am a normal girl, I am a lay woman, don't make it so complicated sweetheart.

Here we are living in the cages, I want to make myself free from all the confinement, restrictions, knots of relations and obligations.

Beautifully Faded

I want to live in a world where nobody judges me, nobody
judges me on the basis of caste, colour, creed, race, sex,
grades, job, beauty, money. Honey!

I want to live in a world where everyone laughs on my jokes,
not on me.

I want to live in a world where people listen to me patiently,
help me to come out of my problems, not make me mental
and eventually prove me insane.

I want to live in a world where people appreciate my talent,
help me to grow, not they get jealous make their team lay
their net, trap me and make me feel so weak that I one day I
hang myself on the fan with the rope and end my story.

Where can I find such a world?

I want to live, I want to live, I want to live…

Anukul Bansal

<u>LIFE</u>

Life is a beautiful master price.

A sketch and that too a empty one

Has been given to all of us.

Fill it with our own colors

Life.

Is poetry in motion?

That has no place to hide

It is a hue in a deep sea.

Life is a beautiful bouquet to get

The fragrance till its lasts.

Every day is brand new start to a single possible opportunity
to fill the form of our lives

With glitter, sparkle and water marks.

Yet life is no wonderful!

Beautifully Faded

Anushya Priyadharshini C

(IG: @anushya_priyadharshini)

<u>LOVE</u>

Love makes two lives into one.
Love turns two dreams into one.
Love brings two unknown family together.
Love unites two lives to give a new soul.

Love will not glimpse orthodoxies.
Love will not glimpse iniquity.
Love will not glimpse enunciation.
Love will not glimpse interim.

Is it the love of the Sun to give wonderful brightness to the
Earth?
Is it the love of the Moon to give glacial coolness to the
Earth?
Is it the love of flowers to give its sweet full honey to bee?
Is it the love of fingers to give its mesmerising music on
instruments?

Of course! Because of Love, The World is still evolving!!!

Love completely makes us to understand each other and
relinquish little things!
And yes, we are in love with pen and paper, to fill a blank
paper with beautiful words through ink!!

Love - the meritorious intuition that appears not only to
humans but to everything, everyone in this world!!!

<u>LIFE</u>

Life is similar to voyage on a closely packed boat in a
beautiful heartfelt deep secret sea.
When an elegant sea is really tranquil,
We'll not sense of floating. We'll adore the breezing air and
movable cloud in the sky!
When an elegant sea is really in turmoil,
We'll be insane and ruin the happiness of others. We are
afraid of swinging or sinking!

Similarly, when an elegant life is really tranquil,
We must cherish our lives to the fullest and fulfill our goal
wholeheartedly.
If we misuse our thoughts, peaceful lives will be lost!!
When an elegant life is really in turmoil,
We must determine to vanquish the quandary.
If something is done in a hurry, it will be in burry!!

The one who understand this, fulfill his goal.
The one who doesn't understand this, unwill his goal.
The one who is in between these two, desperate to find
somewhere to live, he forgets his actual goal.

If we just esteem and do our liability with care,
Live with love without any hatred, LIFE will be more
delightful and beautiful!!!

Beautifully Faded

Arijit Roy

(IG: @always_arijit)

<u>**REVENANT**</u>

I stood still on stilts,

Like a long-billed wading bird,

With my slender legs,

And black plumages all over my body.

The scale like leaves of conifers,

Shrubbed the arillate fruits with unilluminated vectors.

The creepy sketches of backscattering image,

From the eerie silence around created a sacrilege.

The wretched wraith from the uneven moonshine,

And a sleazy setting of blasphemous bleakness took its
time,

To sync in with the epilates,

And cover the dextrphobic periods of damaging detriments,

From levophobic spells of morbid melancholy.

The generic indulgence with ephemeral noir,

Calibrated my silhouette with flair.

I stood there on my stilts,

Grazing on a barren turf with no pasture.

I rummaged for a cloak to cover up the nudity surrounding
me,

Beautifully Faded

I yearned for a sycamore to encapsulate the dead cells
flagging me,

I was tried to be an amoeba with no fodder around me,

I paved a road without sand and gravel,

Configuring a distasteful map of misery.

I drilled holes into darkness to drive away the vermin,

I stood still like an apparition staring at the nadir of
hollowness where there was only unknown figurine.

Rising up time and again from deep gorges and bottomless
chasms,

Shrugging and regaining consciousness from the sporadic
spasms,

Loneliness was the lousy lubricant,

Reducing the friction between my semblance and
substance.

Still I made futile attempts to make up for the blunt
blunders,

Like a bald scalp searching for fallen hairs.

I chased unknown categories,

Traversing different trajectories,

But the onrush of time caught me unaware in its nexus,

Like a gaudy gossamer forming a plexus.

I was in a quest to attain the maximums,

Which was frivolously facetious.

Beautifully Faded

Arnab Kumar Gupta

(IG: @arnabkgupta_create_unleash)

THROUGH ARTIST'S EYES

She, Postured as her feminine best',

Was hypnotic for eyes, unmoved at her beauty's hest,

For they saw her as an enchantress,

Enticed by her heavenly grace!

My hands being insanely instinctive,

Meticulously carved out her curves,

So nubile, eyes so distinctive!

As my pencil stroked her beautiful long hair,

Eyes relished vision of her intricately convoluted ears!

The wrinkles on forehead spoke of her suppressed desires,

Concealed within her exquisite eyebrow's proud attire!

Her long, so elegant, perfect straight nose,

Integrated with luscious lips, gave me a drooling dose!

Caressing the strokes within her face and hair,

Kissing its created replica of the artist's stare,

Beautifully Faded

My hand pencil reached to the centre of the canvas,

While mind profounding into limerence of its new crush,

Just below her neckline so slender, & sturdy,

Shone her bare back, shapely girlish, an artist hand's party,

Secreting her pert, perfect beauteous female bosom,

And deep-seated succulent navel, a man's fetishistic awesome!

Time had no jurisdiction over the passion,

My hands imbibed within the pencil-paper adhesion,

Until it robed her dummy's such desirable butt,

Sketching the darkened shades of her saree's fancy cut!

As my finishing touches, transversed through her hourglass
proportions,

Her dusky skin, the black Kohl in her eyes glistened out of
emotions,

The hours of my hard work & her ceaseless stance,

Had led us into an indecipherable trance,

Causing a strange bond between her immobility and my
hands creative dance,

The Bong's godlike beauty and the artist's eyes romance.

Beautifully Faded

Ashachowdary Undavalli

(IG: @ashachowdaryundavalli)

LOVING YOU IS HEALING

Loving you is a healing...

Behind my laugh

There is a faded part of me

Behind my eyes

There is a ocean filled with tears

Behind my smile

There is a broken piece of me

Behind my silence

There is a incomplete story

Behind my body

There is a soul' trying to heal

Love remains longer in my heart

For the one, who never return...

<u>LOVING YOU IS HEALING</u>

I never know.... Missing you!!!

Cause a deadly pain...

I'm missing you a little, a little too much!

I'm lucky to have at least some memories...

I'm unlucky be so away from you!!!

It's very hard thing to realize.... That...

I'm losing you!!!!

But I think you never valued my pain...

So, I learnt to forget you!!! But,

Time always bringing back your memories...

I'm trying to accept I never meant for you!!

But, still always a part of me will be...

Waiting for you!!!!! Because…

Loving you is healing !!!

Asmi Patel

(IG: @dedicatedtoyou_9794)

<u>YOU</u>

If you breathe, I say you, in every thing you

You are angry and you are the only destination

Neither have you turned your back nor left you

There was no one before you, no one after you

You are the truth and you are the lie

We awakened you in my heart and in my books

The day starts with you and these eyes also close after seeing you

You are my love and you are my escape

Life wants to connect with you and end on you

Have you ever thought of being apart from you, nor of going away from you

You are my nightmare and you are daydreamer

You are my friend and you are the deepest love in friendship

You are my justice and you are my court

You are mine today and you are the one I hide today

Beautifully Faded

You are my crime and you are the witness of my life
Heart was held back

Took care of you
Again I was losing myself to think of you

The heart had already become mad, now life had started
unaccounted for
If you want to find me or lose yourself somewhere in me

There is strength in love that I came with you like this
Otherwise no girl leaves her house for anyone

Love is always with someone
But my story and yours was something else which is going to
be completed today

Sometimes your memories support me, sometimes you
remember me
Everyone's crazy heart is there but not everyone's crazy

Otherwise no love would be incomplete nor any separation
nor any separation is a matter of heart, that's why the world
accepts sacrifice
If there was talk of self-destruction then the destruction
would have spread

Handing the heart that you can tell yourself sometimes
But now books have started getting to know me better

It is heart that your name is chanting and neither the floor
standing in front is visible nor the cheats eaten behind

You have the gurus to love you on your own and also the
experience of listening to the words of others, but still kept
your heart pressed like you did.

Beautifully Faded

Bala Abirami G

(IG: @abijdn6)

<u>TO MY FADING NATURE</u>

Smile of Greenery

Wakes me eagerly...

Calmful cool breeze

Makes me freeze...

Streaming of water

Reflects me brighter...

Blooming of flowers

Gives me showers...

Steep stand tree

Protect me free...

Finding one's soul

Peaceful on whole...

You don't fade away

I can't make a way...

In your lovely World.

Beautifully Faded

REMINISCING MY FADED FATHER

Even mountains would fall apart

With one man's lovely heart...

His hands unfolded my world

My birth would go deserved...

He proffer me all his blood

To frame me strong in flood...

He strives all his struggles

To surprise me with miracles...

My pathway may have footprints

But he upholded all those steps...

Things that I beautifully adorned

For it he himself burned...

With world's words, I can praise

But I can't make him raise...

Still with your heavenly memories.

Baljeet Kaur Virdi

(IG: @baljeetvirdi5)

<u>ANGELS ON EARTH</u>

Not very long but only a little ago,
I was hardened like a stone,
Fallen like a leaf in the autumn,
Yet innocent like a lamb.
I was struggling hard to stand and walk with the world,
But unaware of the goal and the way, I failed to do so.
I cried for help, but every time I was mocked.
Then came the 'Angels' of the Earth,
With calm face and brightened eyes.
Their serene touch comforted me,
And like a true potter, they started moulding me,
Into a tactful, tolerant person.
They introduced me with my inner strength,
And helped me to rise from dust.
They instilled in me the eagerness to learn,
And to soar higher for the new world.
Just like a true companion, they guided me and cared for me,
Teaching me to be humble, like the laden cedar tree,
And working hard like a toiling bee.
Thank you for being the angel of my life,
Guiding me and helping me to rise.

<u>MENU</u>

In the restaurant last evening after a decade,

Remember, you invited me to dine with you?

How excited I was to receive the invitation from you,

Thinking, it would be an exotic moment to meet you.

But, who knew you would be interested only to discuss the
restaurant menu,

When darling, actually I was there only to talk about me-n-u.

Bhagya Sree Nammi

(IG: @ bhagi__shines___)

<u>ME</u>

The me you see today, is different from the me you once
knew....

I no longer worry about my past,

I no longer give a shit about what the society believes,

I no longer give a damn about who is going to judge ,

I no longer strive hard to impress the man I love,

I no longer stay awake and cry all the night,

I no longer fear that you will abandon me one day,

I no longer get depressed by the way you treat me,

I no longer get fooled by your stupid tricks,

I no longer dream and pray to stay by your side,

I no longer think that I'm broken and empty,

I no longer miss you,

I no longer love you....

Instead I love the new me....

I FUCKING LOVE THE NEW ME!!

<u>DEAR NATURE</u>

Dear nature,

Whenever I reached greater heights in life, you showed me mountains, no matter what heights you reach in life remain grounded...

Whenever I worried about my problems, you showed me problem are like clouds they pass away easily.....

Whenever I felt alone, you gifted me the trees, the guiding hands, which helped me in finding my way out through the loneliness....

Whenever I felt ugly, you remind me that even the beautiful butterfly was once an ugly caterpillar...

Whenever I failed, you showed me waves to remind me heights and depths are a part of life...

When my soul leaves this body and when this body begins to rot, when no human dares to sit next by me... I wonder how you are able to merge me within you!!!

Beautifully Faded

Chandrima Das

(IG: @chandrima_writings)

<u>I WILL GO SO FAR</u>

I will go so far, far away,

To the place where I can live alone anyway.

No rules of anything,

I am afraid to realize the painful realities.

I can't find any blissful path,

I only can see some crucial part.

Then I try to imagine some dreams,

I realize the story, its matched with fictitious realities.

I will go so far, where no complications remain,

I am afraid of the illusive path, I'm very sensitive in real.

I will go so far, where expectations will not hurt,

A pure heart always feels more, it's like an art.

I will go far; I don't know the definition of dishonesty.

Dear, do you know? I'm a worshiper of originality!!!

THE CRUX OF SOCIETY

I don't know how to describe the depth of cruelty,

Society is toxic, overpowering people leads the reality.

Its sorrow to hear the painful noise of crying,

When a child abused daily, woman whoever survived.

Women are mothers, children are like God,

But they oppressed for money or physical temptation.

Will anyone shows sympathy to a forced soul ?

Society is infected, everyone is not capable.

Chirag L Sagar

(IG: @chirag_cls18)

TO BEING YOURS FOREVER

My heart resonates with yours when I take a breath,

And I realise that you're right next to me.

Even though we're miles away from each other,

Your thoughts sway in my mind every single moment,

And I feel that you're right next to me.

A day without you feels like an year,

And I turn dull and gloomy.

When I feel your presence,

My heart's floating in cloud nine.

Wish you were next to me.

I'd love to spend my whole life alongside you,

And finally take a last breath holding your hand.

My existence in this world,

Is not at all a coincidence.

I've always had a person in my life,

Whom I love beyond the moon and back.

If I lose you anytime, anywhere,

Beautifully Faded

I'll go against all odds and fight with the world,

To win you back.

The dark rainclouds in the sky,

Are bound together by the threads of love.

The gentle shade that comes up after a round of torrential
rain,

Is a creation of the Almighty to cheer you up.

I dream of nothing,

But staying besides you holding your hands,

Live my life with you,

Until my last breath.

Beautifully Faded

Christina Ekka

(IG: @Craz_ywriter9)

<u>JOURNEY OF MY LIFE</u>

The Journey of my life , with a empty jar on my hand.

Jumping around mud, shipping rocks on the river.

Hiding behind when anger turn around.

Rush on ground, hit on stone, the naughty fights.

Putting laugh and smile in jar to see the dreams so far.

Stepping like a lazy turtle, to work as a craziest leopard.

With full of confidence buring in heart;

Innocence turns into sluts.

Cold drink turns into alcohol

Now eyes were like a old opera tune.

Broken words , buried Heartbeat Faded jeans.

Terrible cries corner of dark room;.

The voice left behind

Chasing a hope light behind,

Like a tiny grain of sand folding away far.

Filling fair, sacrifice and broken beat in jar.

A faded voice rise from behind.

Beautifully Faded

The drew of eyes dried up.

The legs were standing again.

The smiles and laughs were rise up;

The heartbeat of mind again

Breaking the jar of sadness ,cries of corner

Failure of disappointment, mysteries and regret.

Opening the jar of smiles and laughs

Confidence, love and joy around.

Darshika Morey

(IG: @buddingsolace)

<u>THE BEAUTIFUL ROSE</u>

I still have your rose.

Kept beautifully between

Those pages of prose.

It always remind me

of the day we met

And our relationship soared.

It was the day when all the birds

Were singing for us, winds hustling,

As if everyone was trying

To bring us close.

It is the token of our love,

The beautiful Rose!

Still kept between

Those pages of prose

HOW BEAUTIFUL WAS OUR BOND

I use to fear, feared losing you a lot;

That fear let me hold you tighter.

But I forgot, love is not about keeping

The chained heart,

It is about freeing the soul and making it

Fly higher.

Now you are gone,

And I want a chance; once in a lifetime

To move a magic wand,

Spell the words and show you,

How beautiful was our bond!!!

Beautifully Faded

Debanjana Ghatak

(IG: @dgwrites_)

<u>I AM FREE, I AM ME</u>

What would you say if I tell you to smile?

I'll but when I wish.

What would you narrate if I ask you to speak?

I'll but only when my soul commands.

How would you sway if I ask to dance?

Yes, I'll move the way my heart seeks.

What would you do if my words hurt you to cry?

I'll shed but never for you.

Why?

Because I am free, I am me,

I follow my rules and break whenever I wish.

It's my life and

Will lead in my own term.

No one to care,

Don't you dare.

Beautifully Faded

<u>BE YOURSELF</u>

Be Yourself,

Don't Change,

Let the world change for you.

Be Yourself,

Don't Hide,

Let the world learn from you.

Be Yourself,

Always Shine,

Let the world feel proud of you.

Be Yourself,

Keep that Smile,

Let the world rejoice with you.

Be yourself,

Never give up and

Teach the world how to smile.

Beautifully Faded

Deep Mitra

(IG: @badguystolemyusername)

<u>THE HABIT CALLED LOVE</u>

I have seen Lovers

In a romantic relationship

Trying to tick the boxes of expectations

Trying to steer clear of potential conflicts

Trying to hold on to each other

Because they have to

And

Amidst all this

I have seen Love taking a backseat

Just two people losing themselves

In pursuit of something they call togetherness

It's one thing to adjust

To accommodate

To realign according to your partner

A completely different thing though

To lose oneself to the extent of oblivion

Beautifully Faded

Look for someone

Who loves you as you are

Who lets you be your stupid self

One who doesn't try and tame you

Into a timid pet looking for peace

Than love and the adventures accompanying it

For love isn't meant to be sheepish

It can be as wild as your thoughts go

As unchartered as the open sky

As much bound by rules as an unflinching rebel.

Deepjyoti Chowdhury

(IG: @dj_writes_to_heal)

<u>BEAUTIFULLY FADED</u>

That budding love in my heart the moment I saw you,

The feeling was magical and my little heart had no clue.

Those butterflies in my heart were tickling me down my
spine,

In my sweet dream you had already offered me a glass of
wine.

Quietly I sat down hiding my blush and smile,

Soon enough I was in the middle and you were at the aisle.

In this poetry I will try my best to compile,

The way I was completely taken aback by your smile.

Soon I realized you were a part of my team,

With happiness and glee my heart started to scream.

A new feeling I felt in my heart that day,

My mind filled with countless beautiful dreams.

The same feelings you felt in your heart I knew,

The moment you offered me a lift, my mind completely
blew.

Beautifully Faded

My heart was rejoicing and thoughts lost in you,

Yes, "I would come" , I said standing like a statue.

You dropped me home safe and sound,

I felt like a princess who just got crowned.

In those mysterious eyes my little heart got drowned,

Little did I know, I was under some spell bound.

In just a couple of weeks you made me weep,

It was all because I did not let your intention complete.

You wanted me physically but your love was my need,

Every night with a bleeding heart I went to sleep.

One fine night you were finally caught,

I saw you with another girl, exactly what I had forethought;

You claimed you never promised me love with a gnash,

My love and my feelings turning into ash.

With time that hurt beautifully faded,

Penning down my pain and healing souls, my soul got
upgraded!

Deepti K S

<u>LOST IN OUR THOUGHTS</u>

With the flowing time, all of us grow old,
We stop making decisions, that are downright bold.
We often wonder about our lives on a night that's cold,
Gathering all our thoughts together, most of which remain
untold.

There is a part of us we have loved the most,
There is a part of us which we wish, could vanish like a ghost.
We yearn to travel from the seas to the coast,
Where we play the role of the guest and the host.

Our tired bodies and minds need rest to reminisce what we
have left in the past,
To revisit the broken promises and the relationships that
didn't last.
We watch our life go on, sometimes slowly and sometimes
fast,
We stare at what we experienced, through the lens of our
emotions so vast.

While we will always have with us, the treasure of the days
that have gone by,
It's important to move forward in order to dream some more
and fly.
Life is too short to look back and simply cry,

Because in the end, we'll bid all our memories, a well-
deserved goodbye!

A WALK DOWN THE MEMORY LANE

Together, as we take a walk down the memory lane,

Holding our hands, reliving the endless pain;

Recollecting everything that the merciless past did to strain,

Our relationship, so that we never saw each other again.

What I thought would be a journey so beautiful,

Became a battleground with fights really awful;

So much that after a point in time, I lost my cool,

And walked away never to look back, feeling ungrateful.

I may have decided to move on in life, but you chose to
stay,

Holding on to the agony, suffering day by day;

Until one day, you quietly decided to pass away,

One final adieu, is what I didn't get to say.

So when we take that walk down the memory lane,

It'll be not on this earth, but when we meet in heaven.

Devasmita Pathak

<u>SUCCESS</u>

Don't be lazy until you are not succeed,

Don't be sleepy until you are not succeed,

Success is a dream and wish of a person,

But Success do not dream and wish a person,

It is the way which makes us great,

But it is not easy to find it,

It is a passion which makes a person mad,

But the person who has gone mad for success is not really a mad.

<u>MY FRIENDS</u>

They are the happiness,

They are the gladness,

They are the brightness

Of my life...

They are the motivators,

They make me happier,

They are the lighters

Of my life...

They make me feel good,

They make my mood,

It's my goodness

That they are part of my life...

They are the wonders,

They are the wunder,

They are the changers

Of my life...

If my life is a garden than flowers are my friends making
my beautiful and full of fun.

Digya Sinha

(IG: @digyasinha)

<u>GOING & GONE</u>

He was losing it all,

All that he has.

He was going so far,

Far as he can.

He was going in deep,

Deep as he can.

He was going towards the light,

To the light of night.

He was moving away from you,

You and from me .

He was broken in and out,

Still stand loud.

His eyes have no light,

Beautifully Faded

There was night without moonlight.

But he moved on,

On towards the dawn.

Again and again he tries,

He tries to light his life.

He stand to fight,

With that horrible sight.

His soul was now all,

Was ready to be gone.

He was fading it all,

Still was beautifully gone.

Beautifully Faded

Diksha Agrawal

(IG: @t_tales.of.diksha)

<u>OH CYCLE! WE KNOW YOU AS LIFE</u>

Whenever hell came they denied
But their heart spoken
Dark is night, sky is white
Still search for light,

Whenever life turned they denied
But their heart spoken
Skip that one, try next one
Still hope for bright,

Whenever friendships harmed they denied
But their heart spoken
Take your time, everything will be fine soon
Still spend for belief,

Whenever love not find they denied
But their heart spoken
Try to forget, forgive from deep inside
Still open for more hurt,

Nevertheless I think, they all assent with it
But I find, everyday their bliss heart
Allows them twice or although thrice
Take a big slice of laughter,

Yesterday to today, another layer of itself
It shows along with a way of overcome
And that is the reason innumerable dreams
Resides in dreamer's eyes with spirit of do or die.

<u>MY SOULMATE</u>

Be my moon forever

And

Shed light on all my paths like as old days,

You are mine,

You are my firefly from the old days

Who walk with me till today?

But due to days we meet at night

That's why I want.

Your sky!

Dimple Nilesh Gurnani

(IG: @scatteredthoughtsbydimple)

<u>UNSETTLE</u>

Come, unsettle with me

for we can have a small house in a small town

Come, unsettle with me

for we can survive with love with our basic needs

Come, unsettle with me

let's leave behind the world full of show-off

Come, unsettle with me

not everyone needs luxury, I can have you and you can have
me.

Beautifully Faded

<u>MEMORIES</u>

Do you think creating memories hold great pleasure?

Most of the times, it isn't true

Because when time changes, situations change & with that,
people change

And when we don't adapt with these changes, we part ways
from these people who were once important part of our
lives,

And then these memories become suffocating.

Dipika Ghatak

(IG: @breathing_place)

<u>MEMORIES</u>

We lost each other like darkness to light…

Like sand in my hand held so tight…

But memories should fade…

Hope someday it might…

<u>FIRST CRUSH</u>

We first met at a point where you were the only visible priority…

Then the world came around & you faded away in course of my maturity…

But you are still the secret smile…

You are the first crush of the innocent silly child…

Divya Pushparaj

(IG: @eyethought.in)

<u>ITS BETWEEN THEN & NOW</u>

Hey dear & darling then has become

Hi & how are you now!

It was like a day's food, 4 times at call

Has become a hardest diet now!

Sleepless hours of conversing then

Are sleepless hours of mind conversing now!

1000s of thoughts through voice then

Flows through eyes now!

100s of sharing restricts to Share a glance now!

A huge hug then is hesitant to give a smile now!

The craziness then added to hurt makes to ignore u now!

That massive affection then has never faded dull now!

I expect a day to hate you completely

And to retain my happiness or to bring you back!

<u>IMPORTANCE</u>

If someone had been so important to you once?

And they well know that they are your first priority among all beings around you thence!?

You fight damn for their wellness?

Cared them like heaven showers down flawless?!

Yet you are just a check-list for them?

Alas 😃! They miss your kindness and you never miss any of them!

Never hold on for something where you gave all your best, still you end up in tears!

It's not, u deserve for all your affection!

Move forward.

Fathima Ruqaiya Shifan

<u>NATURE</u>

Nature is a wonder,

That makes me ponder,

I am amazed with it,

It really is a beauty kit.

Flowers and trees,

Shakes cold breeze,

What is better ?

Than wondering into nature.

Nature is a guide,

That rides,

In your mind,

For you having to find.

Why could be further ?,

Than having to nurture,

your future,

With nature.

Beautifully Faded

THE PLACE OF WONDER

The cold breeze

That makes me bloom like a flower after a wither,

The sensitive sweetness and your aroma,

As I enter you.

Your tall trees and your green attire,

Having colourful buttons on it matching your clothes,

When I sit on your white strong hair,

I calm down.

You remind me of my great grandma,

Whose massage I always adored,

I sit on her lap and she gently makes me sleep,

The one who left me few years ago.

Your length like a tower,

Your width as a river,

Your words cannot pay any,

Oh! Place I am amazed.

Garima Thukral

(IG: @garima.thukral)

A LITTLE MORE SUNSHINE

Life is beautiful,

Everything so wonderful!

It's time to create your own sunshine,

And hear everyone like a wind chime!

The world seems so divine,

Taking a break from the eternal grind!

Sometimes life defies gravity,

But that's not the tragedy!

Breaking the chains of dark,

Let's carry on with a spark!

With every drop a pearl is born,

Is there really a need to mourn?

I can feel my heart lighten,

And universe so brighten.

When I really began to think,

Everything was dressed up in a golden sheet…

<u>A BEAUTIFUL GIFT</u>

When you smiled at me today,

I started smiling too.

Nothing happens in a day,

I've realized it all through!

You add a spice of fun and an extra ray of sunshine,

Don't know how it all begun,

What God has beautifully designed?

You are a priceless gift,

Who is always admired.

Thankyou for the uplift and taking me higher!

I love it when you embrace me tight,

That makes me forget my fear.

You are a guiding light,

And there is no way i would shed a tear!

You are my need,

When you leave I feel blue.

Along with you I succeed,

And I love you!

Idaya Rani

<u>ALL WITHIN ONESELF</u>

Life is too short, don't brood over something...

It leaves us with nothing...

Create your own world...

That's your eternal shield...

Do live each moment...

Ensure you never lament...

Find what you love...

Then do a deep dive...

Control your anger..

Otherwise it will put you in danger...

Do help those in need..

Always stay from greed..

Never crave for money...

Realize your divinity and change your destiny...

Happiness nowhere else...

All within oneself…

<u>THE VOICE OF SOLITUDE</u>

Talks to me when I stay away from others...

Is it voice of soul? Or voice of mind?

Often feel like I am confined between them...

The war between my rational and irrational thoughts...

I try to run away from it...

I love to connect with people to get rid of it...

But I end up hurting myself more than before...

Shall I go back to my solitude?

I realized the battle within me all for my good...

To evoke the inner energy of my soul...

By thrashing the beast within me

Of my insecurities, fear, despair, hopelessness and
negativity...

Solitude assures me to be my partner forever...

To lead in the path of light when the world of darkness
overpowers me...

The voice of solitude is mellifluous...

Beautifully Faded

Indu Sri Lakavath

(IG: @jzpenningmyfeelings_)

<u>MY LOST MEMORIES</u>

I miss those days,

When I used to reach school on a bicycle;

And returned late due to my friend circle.

I miss those days,

When I used to play with marbles;

And enjoyed their twisting wobbles.

I miss those days,

When reading comics was a naughty deed to my parents;

But enjoying them was one of our loving commitments.

I miss those days,

When I used to watch Doordarshan every night;

And The MahaBhaarat was my favourite.

I miss my days,

When sleeping on mother's lap was my daily routine;

And there was less importance to any machine.

<u>HER UNSPOKEN WORDS</u>

She was born in the poor family,

But she didn't care.

She was brought up with no luxuries,

But she didn't even bother to care.

She was surprised with an unfortunate guest.

This time, she had to care.

He destructed her body with his hands,

She didn't knew how she could handle to care.

He opened the way to depression for her,

But surprisingly, she didn't take it to care!!

When she informed it to her parents,

They asked her not to share it anywhere.

This time, her soul was actually destructed,

She left the world, as her own silence was the one she
couldn't bare.

Let her speak. Let her live. Let the world survive.

Beautifully Faded

Jagdeep Singh

(IG: @_jagdeep_singh_buttar)

<u>OWE IF</u>

suede de erotic, a stoic, et heroic patience,

is zij (she) himalyas?, a pious,

if to odin, a conveyance, ut (to) celes,

driest ses cor, owe if, a atone, thus...

est a pots?, if to besot,

angelic a lip, gossips of rose, soma if prairie,

apres bathes if, en onsen de muscat liquors, devote it tote,

driest ses cor, owe if, a miserere, thus...

gascon aube soloist, to its crescendo,

adjunct solitudes, de poet en woodlot,

if ode?, de aoede,

driest ses cor, owe if, a selichot, thus.

Beautifully Faded

PLEASES

oral guilts of passed afters,

lobbed to erroneous addresses, if,

contagion a erotogenic touches, possesses,

congest perfumes of apropos asters,....

"exegesis of a serious issues,

cessations of coyness, cause unfoldings to egg on,

sees a poet to, 'simultaneous dyad saggy dawns',

accolade a oscilatting tissues,....

"moans of canopies, curtains do scintillating,

recitations to poesy belows,

casing en salts, as for jostling a pillows,

et, sniffing a spring,....

"portraying of poses, enact paradises,

plays of foreplay,

a absenteeism, roses to coquet, or a delay,

goblets of soma, as far pleases.

Jayshree Gore

(IG: @adira1694)

A BEAUTIFULLY FADED DREAM

Some feelings were touched today…

In the midst of the flooded streets…

I was falling in love again (flashback)…

The music was accompanied by his heartbeats. . .

The deep desires came rushing to the surface…

The melted and delicate existence came to life…

Everything we dreamt of was hitting my head again…

Our dream home and me being his wife…

He is revived in my every single thought and dream…

Every rainbow and raindrop bring his heart closer to
mine…

I exist in his every dream, him being awake or asleep at
night…

We are together there in our dreams and rest is just fine…

<u>WHEN WOULD I GET A CHANCE TO SEE YOU AGAIN?</u>

When the sun shines brighter,

When I learn to be a fighter…

When the soil smells sweeter because of rain,

When the eyes run dry after being drenched in tremendous pain…

When the waterfalls are flooded though they are quite and calm,

When in the storm, your hug feels comforting and warm…

When the world is cherished as love flourishes,

When our love is what the nature nourishes…

Joya Barbhuiya

(IG: @writingcorefinder.core)

<u>I AM THE WIND</u>

I move on from high to low,

I pass through coarse with flow,

I am heartless, I am painless,

People may come and go,

I am the wind, I have to flow.

People love me the way they want,

People hate me the way I turn,

I have to move, I have to run,

I love everyone, as they have to breathe in turn,

I am the wind, I have to run.

People can't stay with me,

People can't be with me,

Expectation ruins everything,

But I have expectation for none,

I am the wind, I have to flow I have to run.

Life is a nice play I know

Beautifully Faded

It brings pleasure and pain with flow,

I don't know what I have done ? what I have done?

Life will taught me what I have to learn,

I am the wind I have to flow, I have to run.

Beautifully Faded

K. Jayaprakash

(IG: @Mr_quotes_creater)

THE LOVE I BELIEVE IS

Attractive than Bermuda

Beautiful than Taj mahal

Conductive than silver

Deepest than mariana

Energetic than gamma

Flexible than graphene

Gigantic than bluewhale

Hardest than buckypaper

Iightest than aerogel

Joyful than finland

Kindest than capybara

Loyal than dog

Mysterious than blackhole

Narrow than magnesium

Older than pyramid

Powerful than illuminati

Quietest than antarctica

Resistive than glass

Stranger than atlantis

Beautifully Faded

Transparent than zblan

Unstable than francium

Vivid than heather

Wider than universe

Xeric than Atacama dessert

Yummier than briyani

Zillionaire than Jeff bezos.

Beautifully Faded

Kawal Bakshi

(IG: @alfazo_ke_ruh_)

<u>SCARS OF LOVE</u>

Love can profound in the darkness of hope

You just need to behold yourself toward the ray of hope

Soul will internally believed the dark shades of love

Still we all fall for someone who never meant for us

We make yourself a butterfly who easy to catch by holding
their wings

Never give province to anyone who holds u tight

Every cloud in the sky needs the air right

Who made you worthless by giving favor to love?

Always have concern towards the matter of naive

Hiding the things never be a part making the things
working have make heart

Fly higher in the sky with wings never settle down

Shades of love always bring u on height

Choosing the shape of yourself not hidden in woods

It's always be good to having the faith in goddess

Purity never be dull by someone thoughts

Always see yourself from the eye of your known

Take a walk with a glimpse of light

Never hold yourself tight

Beautifully Faded

The day we met stars starts falling from the sky

The shadow of our smiles became light

You hold my hand tightly no air would pass through it and
chuckles softly

The way u looks into my eyes and shows me that u has
everything u want

My sorrows behind my joy u will always finding soon

When I met u I always said I want moon

Ur heart start beating fast like the horse in the race

We make so many castles in the air under the moonlight

We never left anywhere our love trace

Promises u always kept the dreams on which we work

The grudges we hold stronger than our bond

Never u made the things on hold

Recalling memories day and night

I always knew your love make everything right.

Beautifully Faded

Keerthana R

(IG: @claiming_me_a_scribbler)

<u>LOVE ON FIRST SIGHT</u>

With my coiffure mushroomed and schoolbag heavy

My joy dazzled visaging his hair bonny

With my deep tubby blow and heart hefty

My glory havened glancing his chin cheery

Yes, it's my beautifully faded one!!

With my uniform grey and eyes pink

His watch portrayed romantic with shirt blue

With my laces loose and lips abuse

His tie was tight with face clean white

Yes, it's my beautifully faded one!!

Waiting for my school bus arriving nine thirty nine

His Innova horned tight posing nine twenty five

Hustling my eyes for a glance twilight

His blink invoked my iris, a glamorous light

Yes, it's my beautifully faded one!!

His glance was light which my nerves caught fright

Beautifully Faded

His smile was bright, evoking my heroine alight

With his nose small sharp and lips red blood

My soul was ready, in spite being, a minor teddy

Yes, it's my beautifully faded one!!

With his name unknown and place unaware

Desiring for his hug, next hundred years alive

My love on sight was bright catching height

Panicking about his reply, mum I lie

Yes, it's my beautifully faded one!!

With bus horn massive, taking me away, spontaneous,

My heart squirreled weighty, for next meet hungrily

Unaware of my upcoming, I needed him badly

Years passed, waiting and waiting, for him lovely

Yes, it's my beautifully faded one!!!

Beautifully Faded

Kishore Karuthiruman

(IG: @kishorejeevi)

<u>TOGETHER FOREVER</u>

Hearts are like sparks.

When they fly, they ignite.

Eyes are like stars.

When they strike, they shine.

Thoughts are like dreams.

When they come up, they penlights.

You are like moon.

When it's full, I feel complete.

I am like scars.

Cause moon has scars.

They both are together,

Actually forever..!!!

<u>ONLY IF YOU UNDERSTAND MY HEART</u>

Only if you understand,

I would have given you more signs,

Of me wanting to love you.

Only if you understand,

You would notice my eyes,

When they glance at you.

Only if you understand,

You would have known,

That you are special to me.

And

Only if you understand,

You would have heard

My "I LOVE YOU".

Beautifully Faded

Kohima

(IG: @kohgirlpower)

Living in the chaotic world,

I search for the, rays of love

I search for the, rays of purity

I search for the, rays of kindness

I search for the, rays of warmth

I search for the, rays of truth

I search for the, rays of compassion

Yes, living in the chaotic world,

I search for all this.

But,

It makes me tired,

It leaves me broken,

It tends to doubt my own self,

It makes me to introspect,

It leaves me by my own self.

Searching for all this,

One day I stop.

Beautifully Faded

But do you know what happened,

I grew up with what I search for,

I possess what I want to see outside,

I collect all the rays within myself,

What I searching for,

Beautifully shined in me,

Which was faded outside.

Beautifully Faded

Meenakshi Binani

(IG: @meenakshibinani)

<u>PAPA</u>

I don't often tell you, but I love you

Reluctant, rebellious, fierce and stubborn I might be

But your daughter won't let u down

Pardon my silly crime

Hold on this "one last time"

Each day I'm struggling to be little lot like you

Striving hard to be your pride

Thanks, for always being by my side

Not ultimately but definitely!

I'll be as great as you

Paa… I don't often tell you, but I love you.

Beautifully Faded

<u>SANGUINE</u>

Lonely, sad, lost and despair…

Remember:

It's the burning sun that glare

It's okay, if he doesn't like you,

Your prince charming is somewhere waiting for you

If they bully you, laugh along

It will turn them to stew

Fat- thin, Short-tall, fair-dark-- doesn't describe you

It's your smile that beautifies you

Look at the mirror, to find the "best"

There's no comparison with the rest.

Beautifully Faded

Megha Tamang

(IG: @m_e_g_h_a_tamang)

<u>WILL I BE THE SAME AGAIN</u>

Those sleepless nights turning into frightening morning,

days were passing when this soul was still alive, but in your
memoirs, burning alive.

Do you care to think of hurt you gave me and ripped this
heart to think it's all right?

Do you hear the sound of my hopes breaking like the
landfall?

My Pillows soaked in the dreams of your happiness & our
togetherness,

The inner me swears those feelings for you have always been
more,

Did you even try to feel those untold words of mine, when
you left me behind?

Did you ever wonder the depth of my pain is deeper than the
ocean veins?

Admits my soul, this beating of my hollow chest, like
heartbeat without a heart.

it was and had always been me, never did you ever pass away
and make me live my sins.

Why did you tend to shower those unasked concerns?

Beautifully Faded

When you are the one not to bother any of my sense.

Why didn't you just leave me alone, still a part in me only
want you so long.

Years passed, and this stubborn piece of my mind stuck out
to be the same,

still shedding over salted drops, being envious on seeing you
with any other frame.

Was that you who walked past me in that metro train, without
any glimpse of my presense.

Was that you with whom I've always smiled all night while
long silly talks and never felt this awesome of that your body
fragrance.

Peers have had their lots, trying to delete you out of my all
pains.

Will I ever be this insane for someone, now that you are
gone,

Will I ever let this heart to open its doors and allow someone
else to come again?

Dark circles around my eyes, and those dried lips are yet to be
stained.

aboding anyone but you, my heart is quite out of trend.

Can I smile at your silliness just the way I used to do?

Can I just hold you in my arms, the way I had dreamt in my
dreams which is all about you?

Beautifully Faded

Meghana Dumpala

(IG: @so_felt_feelings)

<u>RED SWEATER</u>

Walking on the winter roads

In the snow filled streets

Wearing my red sweater on

Waiting on the winter roads

Under the snow filled umberella

Wondering if we have anything in common

Wandering in your warm thoughts

In the frosty winter breeze

Wishing your presence in person

Whipping off by the icy winds

In the chilly winter nights

Wondering if you'll ever meet me in person

Wilting off in the cold winter

I saw you in the snow filled streets

Wearing the same red sweater on.

<u>MY MISERABLE FATE</u>

I sink into the night

And swim in the dark

Coz in the world of the light

Many have souls of the dark

I drown into the ocean of sorrows

And float over the betrayal

Coz in the world of light

Many are the knights of betrayal

I mourn on my own fate

And regret my life

Coz in the world of light

No one really cares…

Beautifully Faded

Miriam Michaiel

(IG: @avimiri_raj)

THE VOICES OF INNOCENT

Why being forced, why not hear our voice,

Can't we be treated equally and respected!

It doesn't mean you have the right to take

advantage, on the fragile one's.

Arrange marriage held for a very young age,

Favourable or against it, who will care?

Rituals and preparations take place,

But, what about those girls,

as I am sure they'll be scared.

They are like a blooming flower,

Flourishing the world.

Leave it alive free and alight.

Don't let their inner die, but

Make these innocent voices

Wild and aloud.

<u>EVERYDAY ROUTINE</u>

I dream of a day

When there's no need to hurry,

In my perfect day,

I don't need to worry.

I watch from my bed

As the sun rises high,

I sit and I look,

At the birds as they fly.

Everyday the sun rises,

Everyday the birds fly.

But I don't seem to notice

and I ask myself why.

Is it because of my daily routine?

Everyday the same thing,

You know what I mean!

Beautifully Faded

Mom Das

(IG: @momishadas)

<u>HIRAETH</u>

To income bed of roses

Going through its prickers,

A way might be bloodshed

Or might filled with soothed

Solitude, where strangers gonna

Accompany you as so-called friend!

Unknown about almighty's end, Longing for homeland,
never to return.

Beautifully Faded

<u>LAWS OF NATURE</u>

I was going close

To explore; Dreams

Were like real,

Catching up the hills, discovering

New-wide earth which came

To me showing light in air.

But everything has to go wrong

As fair follows worst

So am I, was stolen from me

And left alone.

Muktadirr Zaman

<u>JUNGLE OF DREAM</u>

I was in a jungle

When my eyes opened I was in marvel.

I saw the most beautiful but violent sight,

I felt like I am in a world of opposite.

My eyes became blank,

Mangoes are falling from grapes plant.

Elephant's were like small hen,

Ants were probably a big train.

Tigers are running, afraid to see a Deer,

Monkeys are drawing their picture.

When the time of dream was end,

I saw myself not in jungle but in my bed.

<u>LONELINESS</u>

Loneliness is a state of being where,

A subtle piece of dark cloud appears in our emotions.

And after sometimes,

When the cloud lose its power to bring the emotions,

Emotions dropout from our eyes.

Beautifully Faded

Neel Mitra

(IG: @feel_the_neel)

<u>SAUDADE</u>

And if I ever have to choose

Between your freedom and

Having you to myself in my kingdom

I would choose your freedom

With every bit of my wisdom

But with this faint little hope

That maybe I could keep you close

For a little longer, even if not forever

For about this fact, I won't lie

That I think of you as selfishly mine.

Beautifully Faded

Neha Gupta

(IG: @neha_91201)

<u>RAIN – A PAIN</u>

You fall like a pearl in the ocean,

Like a drop of emotion,

Like the tears in my eyes,

And that's the place where you lie.

Rain is not always

A sign of love and emotion.

It can be a melancholy

Song of pain and separation.

You come and fall silently

Over the autumn leaves,

You take away with yourself

All sorrow and nature's grieves.

Breeze blows with your arrival,

Birds sing and peacock dances.

But once again you'll go

Leaving behind sadness and grievances.

<u>WHY DON'T YOU</u>

Why don't you cure,

When I am in pain?

Why don't you shower?

When I need rain?

Why don't you come near,

When I go far away?

Why don't you hear,

When I am silent?

Why don't you wake,

When I am sleepless?

Why don't you feel,

When I am senseless?

Why don't you make me smile,

When I am crying?

Why don't you understand that

With my every breath I am dying?

Beautifully Faded

Nishi

(IG: @nishipoetry)

<u>A LOVE LIKE NO OTHER</u>

Do you even know my love for you?

Ohh, I love you in and out

Sham and candour

Enticing and nasty

Do you listen?

The torment of my renouncing

Of loving you wasn't a flower bed

Wasn't a passage of thorns either

Do you even care?

The roses you gave me were red

My favorites were pink always

The redness, reminded me of the blood

Of my vanquished dreams

Pink is my sky, Pink is me.

So I loved you like no other

Beautifully Faded

I loved you, to be with you

I loved you, for what you were

Saint and felony, both confided in you

So I chose you, above all

For you became my "Heroin" and "Grass"

You flow in my veins and blood

Lingers on my breath

Resistance is impossible

It's only "Death", to do us apart

A love like no other!

Osho Sambit Mishra

(IG: @oshosambit)

<u>CONSENT FOR HEARTBREAK</u>

The sky is blue,
Your words seemed true.
I wonder what lies
Beyond the lies,
That speaketh from your eyes.
These lies are probably gonna break our ties.
I am scared to defy,
The principles I have kept so high.
But I also don't want to sacrifice
The bond we have.
I had travelled across the seven seas,
Several times,
To survive the cheat ,the betrayal
Beyond the rationale.
I wanna simply gaze at your smile,
But sadly it is not justified.
My conscience keeps poking me
And in my heart the pangs arise.
Can I just shut my eyes?
I can,
But will my conscience compromise?
I doubt that.
I can't live,
Nor can I die.
There is a consent required for physical ties.
Then why not for an emotional one, why?

Beautifully Faded

The words, 'I love you' are not enough.
Not enough to make me forget,
How we both lied on the bed.
I was writhing in pain as my anesthesia wore off.
Moaning your name,
Hoping you would hear my shrieks of pain.
But all of it was in vain.
As you were lying in someone else's arms, in his bed,
Moaning his name.
But I dared to ask why,
And,
You gave pathetic reasons for all your lies.
Protecting me? I guess you just wanted to hide.
We don't need consent to break someone's heart,
I just wanna ask, why?

Pavithra S Hegde

(IG: @pavithra6648)

<u>IMPERMANENCE</u>

You are new again.

You will never be the same again.

Every single day a cell dies in your body,

Let, you rejuvenate, rejoice and embody.

So you are new again,

You will never be the same again.

As your thoughts, ideas and emotions keep changing.

That they know they are in the ride of chasing.

Why you hold them, chase them?

And feel burden! Let you free them.

So you are new again,

You will never be the same again.

The situation in which we all are in today is temporary.

Find ways to be constructive, hopeful and thoughtful let, you evolve yourself,

By giving up which made you sick.

So you are new again,

You will never be the same again.

You are god's will,

So keep up your goodwill.

Beautifully Faded

Know the creators rule of 'Impermanence'.

For sure he will bring the dawn of newness.

Let's work as a whole.

As you are new again,

You will never be the same again.

Beautifully Faded

Pooja Khurana Dhamija

(IG: @author_pooja.khurana)

<u>BROKEN RULES</u>

Dear Dad

Sorry, I am breaking the rules.

When I was growing up

I felt enthralled to see the flames fighting with yellow
purple colors.

You stopped me saying Cooking is not for you. You might
burn yourself.

I saw the dew drops falling on the dirty plates and spoons.
Mom bathe them in soapy bubbles they came out new.

You stopped me saying dish washing will hurt your soft
hands.

I saw clothes twirling in the froth of colored water on and
on.

You said washing clothes is not your job.

All I want to see you happy and dancing

not burning yourself behind the flames of daily chores.

You are my princess.

But dad I am breaking your rules today.

As I handed over my crown to my man.

I have to cook

Beautifully Faded

I have to wash.

Not to hurt myself down but to help lift my man.

sorry dad. For the very first and might be many times you
will see me breaking those rules you made to protect me,
but trust me you will be my king forever and I shall smile
any which way to help you smile when you see me.

Yours loving Daughter.

Beautifully Faded

Prachi Mane

(IG: @Soulgram11)

<u>SHE, THE UNBREAKABLE</u>

She is the sea beautiful to watch but dangerous to mess with,

She has that competence which cannot be defined in any length or width,

She is an epitome of love and warmth

She sometimes can be cold, composed and calm,

She can fill your veins with adventure but dare you belittle her and she'll demolish you with her roaring storm,

Conformists says "Treat her right and she can die for you "

But She says, "Treat me right and I 'll live for you",

No hails, no thunderstorm can break her spine

With every passing day She shines like an old wine,

She is that warrior whose battles never end

She, your mother, your daughter, your wife, your friend

A nature's creation which is impeccable

Yes, you are right I am talking about her

SHE, THE UNBREAKABLE.

Prince Chordia

(IG: @prince_chordia03)

A BROKEN GUY AND AN ANGEL

One evening in the park,
He saw an angle;
She was unreadable,
But still, he couldn't resist
He was scared for the first,
Because once he had worst past with one angel;
Still, her aura was mysterious,
Which made him more curious towards her,
She was full of attitude,
Which use to make her more attractive;
But she was a broken angel,
Hidden behind the fake world
She was different,
Still, he fell in love with her;
So, he decides to tell his feelings,
But she rejected him ruthlessly;
Scratching his heart, left no hopes for healings,
As she didn't want the same thing to happen has before in
her past,
And moved away;
So again, he was left broken who walked,
All alone with pain and by hiding behind the world,
Which again make him heartless.

Beautifully Faded

<u>NEVER GIVE UP</u>

Never Give up

No matter how difficult it seems to be.

As it is

Meant to be achieved by you

Never Give up

On the harsh way of success.

If you do so

Then life would be the greatest mess.

Never give up

If you fail once

Don't just start crying.

Remember that one, who fails,

Always achieves.

All the great persons,

Did at least fail once.

Just because they didn't give up,

They shine like a star.

If in your life,

You undergo some pain.

Please don't give up,

Just think once why you have started,

Just try till you succeed.

Priyanka Deshpande

(IG: @deshpriyanka2020)

<u>WHERE LOVE RESIDES</u>

They want to caged me

They want to tie me

All laws and restrictions are imposed on me

But let someone tell them I am bound to be free

I am here to be shared, cared and distributed among others

Yes, I am here to stay

But not as force

But with my Persona

And I am named as "Love"

And I stay only there where

I am accepted, shared, cared, spread and not humiliated

And yes,

I am unconditional.

Beautifully Faded

Priyanka Rajput

(IG: @priyanka_royal_rajput)

SISTERHOOD

Ever since I remember, I only remember listening

Boys knows the friendship, Girls only know bitching

Male friendship worth praising, whereas female friendships

are brooding

Men got the legend of Krishna-Sudama and Karna-

Duryodhan

Women got nothing but epic of beauty which leads to her

victimization

Oppressed reality doesn't change the fact there's no match to

a female pact

Bromance can never overcome the ardor of romance;

Sisterhood can any day surpass the pangs of romance

Men can't skip the female angle when together, though

women forget men's existence when having slumber.

Compliments from guys are great but real satisfaction is when

a girl appreciates

No secret comes out of sisterhood, not even after booze

To burst your bubble and to make no trouble

Every guy may or may not have the best men in life to be

gleeful

Beautifully Faded

But every girl got at least one girl who's always there to make
every sorrow little less painful and happier time much more
cheerful.

Contrary to belief and to major relief

If Arjun has the Krishna there always has been and will be
one Trijata for every Sita.

Beautifully Faded

Rakesh Kumar Sahu

(IG: @r_k_s_28)

THE FALLEN FLOWER

Flower,
A sign of beauty
A symbol of grace
Its pride runs strong
At a very fast pace.
Flower,
Gives birth to fruit
Such parents are like flower
They are everybody's will power.
Flower,
It exudes fragrance
It gives pleasure
It fights with storm
But seems to be danced with breeze.
It sacrifices all for others
After shedding,
Lying untouched and unseen forever
Leaving back its beauty and purity.
After falling,
It's dragged, scratched and crushed
Yet no objection and no accusation.
In its sacrifice,
There's no certain limit
Homeless, nameless, lifeless
Like an extinct.
Always it gave away all it had

Beautifully Faded

There's no corner,
Where it's voice to be heard.
The beauty of the flowers
Before they fall away,
The fragile sweetness, the pleasant color
The worth of love was cruelly paid.
It gets huge appreciation during age young
Time passes away and
Gradually the distance becomes long.
It spends so many nights with
Wind, rain and frost,
But later
No-one is ready to understand its cost.
It gets continuous obstacles
Still it smiles,
As its sacrifice incomparable.
Flowers do everything for the rest
But the rest crush it with feet,
Parents give everything to bairns
But bairns kill all their happiness.
It never cares the cruel sun
And spreads its smell through diffusion,
Such whatever may be the reason
The parents never blame a son.
Flower is the fruit's mother
No doubt,
Parents are living God
With charming color.
Everybody has to face the fate
Of a fallen flower,
But we should be as sacrificing as
A flower.

Beautifully Faded

Rianka Sarkar

(IG: @sarkarrianka)

<u>CRYSTAL</u>

We sat by each other

in brooding silence

He gave me a diamond

I pushed him a laptop

The cake arrived,

Cut in a jiffy

All cameras flashed and clicked

As we danced, kissed and posed

I wore a designer gown

My hands were manicured

My hair-do took two hours

so did my makeup artist

He was late from office

So hurried in his favorite suit

We gave marriage advices

And set couple goals

Beautifully Faded

Dinner time was announced
A sumptuous buffet was served
When the guests had departed
We unpacked their gifts

And when all were gone
We retired to bed
I turned on the side and slept
He opened his laptop.
To finish the pending works,
Happy crystal anniversary to us.

Rose Kumari

(IG: @mortiferous_me)

<u>A MILLIION RIDDLES YET TO BE SOLVED</u>

Every Person is a Riddle to be solved…

Just be at my side I swear I will accept You as You are,

I may ask sometimes for the Moon but could be Happier with the Star,

I'm Not what Everyone feels like,

You need time to have Me in My Actual Avataar,

If I call your names in My Closed-ones,

It's a promise I won't let you go far..

This is exactly how I'm, Now tell me- How You are??

Rutuja Ajit Vasave

(IG: @rutuja.vasave)

<u>SEASON OF SPRING</u>

When the season of spring blooms in the heart,

Color should come in love

Why should the world fight while filling color in love?

Don't go for less than your full potential,

Don't look at me with that love,

The song should match the meaning of wordless love,

When the season of spring blooms in the heart,

Color should come in love.

Why should the world fight while filling color in love?

Petal-petal blooms filled with love,

Whole earth is sealed with the mist,

This color should come in the eyes of youth,

This intimate bath of love bond in comfort,

When the season of spring blooms in the heart,

Color should come in love.

Why should the world fight while filling color in love?

Beautifully Faded

Sadhna Kashyap

(IG: @loveholic_quotes)

<u>CORONA TIMES</u>

Life to a standstill,

The happy states with a sense of misery.

A disease knocked,

And greeted every traveler on its way.

Filling up graveyards,

Where the bodies lay dumped like garbage.

Hunger rained heavy,

On the families with poor little houses.

Masses died with pandemic,

While some died of crawling stomachs.

Hope stood at the ICU,

Breathing slowly to make the sun shine.

The homes were cages,

Everyone prayed,

To make it out alive of this fierceful storm.

<u>WHAT IS RELIGION?</u>

What is Religion? I wish to know,

Is religion the festival of human blood.

I wonder who created the religion?

The fact to divide humanity into halves.

They say religion is about God,

But is god so cruel to his dear children?

Allah, God, Bhagwan are they different?

Or the same person know by many names?

People slaughter each other in riots,

Is it what you call your religion?

I know God doesn't need a permanent address,

To stay in temples, mosques or churches.

He stays within our soul in form of kindness,

But if the kindness is long dead in our soul,

Can God be alive in our religion?

Sagar Bompada

(IG: @sagar_bsv)

Wish you were here, As days became clear

Wish you were here, As I kept holding you dear

Wish you were here, As my heart fills with tears

Wish you were here, As sadness shifted a gear

Wish you were here, As my fears adhere

Wish you were here, As this pain severs

Wish you were here, As no one endears

Wish you were here, As you are my elixir

Wish you were here, As you are nowhere near

Wish you were here, As I lost you last year

Wish you were here, As I can never be insincere.

<u>ADIEU</u>

Haunting memories in my mind

And an irrespirable fate that binds

Joyful times and events rewind

The reality of events hit me like a whirlwind

Deep in my heart, I hold all the love

But the truth comes from the eyes above

As you are nowhere to be seen

I filed my life with caffeine

Every day I ask the god

Why he took you before the nod

Deep in my soul your lovelies

It will not falter until my demise

I'm truly blessed for you in my life

The only regret is I can't make you my wife

Deep in my heart, I hold on to you

As I bid you the final adieu!

Saloni Sahoo

(IG: @salonisahoo)

<u>DEPRESSION</u>

Depression captures the mind of the victim,

Giving him experiences highly unpleasing.

He feels himself being trapped,

And this disease leaving his mind cracked.

He experiences an emptiness,

Being constantly surrounded by sorrowfulness.

How can he live his life?

When for him each day is a deadly strife.

He starts depending on others for happiness,

Having little known that this world is full of selfish people
without much sentiments.

Day by day he finds himself more lonely,

Growing suicidal thoughts in his mind silently.

A day comes when he finally surrenders,

Being forced by this disease to commit this blunder.

He gives up and commits suicide,

Without letting the world know about his depressed side.

<u>ACID</u>

All dreams are shattered with that splash of acid,

Turning face into a state of morbid.

Heart is broken,

Leaving the victim forever grief-striken.

She becomes hopeless,

Simultaneously turning lifeless.

She lacks courage to fight,

To stand against the wrong and the might.

She becomes voiceless,

In a society which is crowded with people rude and
emotionless.

How can she stand up again?

With a heart which is deeply hurt and shaken.

She can hear voices all around,

Mocking, jeering and satirizing her so loud.

But one day she rises,

Overcoming all the depressing causes.

Samshok

(IG: @nick9_5)

<u>BEAUTIFULLY FADED</u>

Today, My love,

Cloud painted the sky so beautifully,

The sun set so gloriously, The moon reappear with billions of stars in the sky tonight and Mark this day to be remembered.

Walking upon this broken path

I shall remember the oath that I took,

To make you laugh in your worse days and to be your comforter.

I'm right here still waiting patiently.

My love, even if you forsake me

I still will wait for you, perhaps was born to love you this way. Angel of love, hear my cry, For I am beautifully faded in love.

Intoxicated on the modern culture she walk,

Expensive food filled her stomach but her heart hungry.

The modern culture blind her eyes and fooled her heart away.

She heard no one and accept no one,

Beautifully Faded

She believed in outer beauty when she's broken inside, she
blindly follow, she blindly believe, believe that she to is
born to be like this, Stop.

Modern culture, what have you done!

She's hurting, she's crying, she's screaming but have you
also unheard her? Just like that, she Beautifully faded.

Beautifully Faded

Sana Kauser

(IG: @mai_teri_shayari)

HELLO MY HEART BREAKER

I may be mad,

But you are always on my mind!

Why do I see you in my dreams,

When you are the one who broke my heart!

I'm so glad you are not the only one,

In this so-called world, selfish one!

Why don't you stop appearing in my life,

As I know this is nothing but a faith!

I curse you a little more,

I don't want to act like a stupid anymore.

You made me fool,

And I lost my youth.

O baby, now don't make a puppy face,

I will ditch you and make you like a crawling snail.

Beautifully Faded

You are nothing but a nightmare in my day,

I always act to sleep whenever I'm in pain.

Sanchari Chowdhury

(IG: @sanchdiary)

<u>FAREWELL</u>

A day that will come in your life for sure,

A day from when you have to say that I was a student of this college,

A day from when there's no more waiting for an another semester,

A day before that day you never realize you will miss this place that much,

A day when you started missing each and every moments you spent here,

A day when your eyes are full of tears but you can't cry,

A day when you find that sometimes it's hard to say a goodbye.

<u>SUPPORT</u>

When you are sad,

But your mom understand that even seeing your face,

And say "what's happened, tell me".

That's called support for me.

When you are struggling with your thoughts,

Your father keep his hand on your shoulder,

And say "what's happened, tell me".

That's called support for me.

When problems that you can't share with your parents,

But there's your best friend beside you,

And say " what's happened, tell me."

That's called support for me.

Sometimes we need a support indeed.

Beautifully Faded

Sangeeta Karmakar

(IG: @sangeetakarmakar)

EVER YOU THOUGHT?

Ever you thought this time will come,

while Earth in motion,

people will be stumped,

having a notion,

how to disconnect

the expanded connection.

Dust departing,

feathers flying in,

chirpings that was missed,

came as a King.

The happiest in the house

is the most loyal being,

look behind the car,

you will find him craving.

Treasuries are running empty,

going high now looks dirty,

Beautifully Faded

one on arm, one walks slow

vanishing like Flamingo.

Behind what is happening

the Little one is cherishing,

holding both Big hands

just wants to dance.

No more holds, no waiting,

when He is singing,

She is bringing,

plum cake with ice dusting.

Beautifully Faded

Saranya Madi

(IG: @daffodil_saranya)

<u>LET'S GO</u>

Let's go,

Whispered the wind to me

And I let my soul fly with glee.

Let's go,

Said my imagination to me

And I set it free.

Let's go,

I heard the sky silently saying me

How I expanded my creativity, consciousness and embraced

It's vastness happily.

Let's go,

I continue to shed my inner mask

to disappear and reappear

When I hear my inner voice say,

"Come along with me forever".

<u>TELL ME</u>

Tell me,

Will you breathe for me,

When I won't breathe,

Run away or hold me close

When I'll be collapsing?

Tell me,

Will you love me,

When I would hate myself,

Leave or Clutch my hands,

When they'll be trembling?

Tell me,

Will you get my mind home to my body,

When I would not be me,

Release or Stabilize, in my veins,

When anxious blood will be flowing?

Beautifully Faded

Sathya Muthu

(IG: @__poetic__vibes)

HIDDEN LOVE

I loved you,

For who you were.

I loved you,

For your laughter and wisdom.

I loved you,

For your uniqueness and flaws.

For the first time had I felt a vibe so different.

For the first time had I wondered so deep.

I was so busy wondering,

That never did I find a time so perfect

To question, if you too loved me .

And now I see myself dejected and silly

As I see you with somebody else,

But my love for you is constant

Only the moments have faded.

<u>DON'T DRINK</u>

A family I knew

Once lived in harmony

Until their father

Fell prey to alcohol addiction

And turned their future bleak.

That's why I say,

Don't drink, you'll sink

And If you sink,

Your family will shrink.

And if your family shrinks,

Your own cohort will find you sick

And will soon kick you out.

So for the sake of yourself,

Stop drowning into drinks

And gift yourself a smile of loved ones,

With your good deeds.

Beautifully Faded

Satyaranjan Mohanty

(IG: @satyaranjan.mohanty)

<u>SINGLE MOTHER</u>

In the name of love

She got betrayed

The one she trusted so much

Gave her a lot hatred.

To raise her baby

She had to struggle

Under the taunt of the society

Never did she crumble.

From morning till night

She fights for her right

Forgets own happiness

To make child's future bright.

The child is growing without father

That thought makes feel guilty

But providing the best

Never makes her faulty.

Which school to join

And which friends to make

Beautifully Faded

Taking all the decisions

She never gets a break.

She carries all loads

Which should be done by two

Who else can handle such pressure

Just like a single mother do.

Starting from love and care

Ending with entertainment

She has to think about

All the society's judgement.

When the child is near, she never bothers

Because she is an independent single mother.

Beautifully Faded

Sayani Giri

(IG: @sayanigiri)

<u>LIFE ISN'T EASY</u>

To walk hand in hand is not easy,

To be with someone all the life is not easy,

But still, life goes on

Whether we want or not

It does not care if you are sad or happy

It does not care if you can bear it or not,

It goes on and on like the flow of a river,

It's constant and unpredictable and maybe

That is why living life isn't easy.

<u>HOW WOULD IT BE</u>

Ever thought how it would be to live

Without a sky, blue as the water of the sea

Without grass, green as the nature itself

Without the sun, moon or the stars to give us light,

Life would be nothing and we would all be

In dust, buried before we could even know to live.

Beautifully Faded

Shahrin Anjum

(IG: @shahrin_anjum)

EMPTINESS OF A GIRL

Every color is filled in my life,

But there is still some color left,

Everyone is with me,

But still someone is with the rest,

I've got entangled in life,

I ask myself to find out the address of pleasure,

Such a catastrophe was not seen,

Some strange heart discomfort,

Yes, this girl is now alone.

Imprisonment is in tears,

Don't know how to shed it,

Intelligence is visible, but

Regenerate the inside but

I don't have a Sick mind but a sick body,

I am happy that god has testing my loyalty,

What do I talk about

Ever so jerk inside my heart

The cemetery of dreams is kept over.

Beautifully Faded

The Trembling lips called many of the 'tales',

but still some of the terms are left.

You have walked just a little away,

The whole cemetery remains ahead.

No one is here to Share my thoughts,

Clouds of sorrows are in my heart,

But I can't see a Drop of rain since a decade,

Do not panic a dark night have to come,

You are just a little away from the beginning,

THE WHOLE CEMETERY IS STILL LEFT.

Beautifully Faded

Shaista Nazir

<u>FILL MY GLASS</u>

Fill my glass

Fill my glass with water

For my destiny resides very farther

Fill my glass with wine

For my haters I have to shine

Fill my glass with a chocolate shake

For my dreams, i have to wake

Fill my glass with a hot milk

For i have to take a perfect click

Or try to fill my glass with poison

I will not step back without a reason.

<u>BELIEVE IN YOURSELF</u>

Believe in yourself

Believe in me

Or believe in you

Believe for the few

who adore what you do

Promise to me

Or promise to you

Promise it now

Each ups and downs you going to love

Share with me

Or share with you

Share with the one

Who won't make it fun

Wait for me

Or wait for you

Wait for your success

To make it endless.

Beautifully Faded

Shyamji Verma

(IG: @shyamjiverma)

<u>CHANGE</u>

Nature has its own game

Which is very strange

It has its own fame

Namely so called 'change'

After birth everything has changed

Including earth from dead to live

From anger to love, making easy to survive

Inorganic to organic, making everything alive

Change is not only related to earth

It may be a signal from subconscious to conscious, costing
little precious

Humans have also changed

Due to some situation or condition

It maybe the respect or greed

Or the lust present in the breed

Everything have two sides

There is nothing to hide

Beautifully Faded

Change is good change is bad

Due to change many are afraid

Change has evolved virtuality

Far away from reality

Making hard to find singularity

Change have made worst into best

Weaker to strongest, weaker from strongest, For many
change is best

For many change is waste

Change has converted earth into mother

Change has evolved a crime called murder

Yes, its change

I know it's strange

For change let us pray

Consider change only in your way.

Beautifully Faded

Smriti Rai

(IG: @smriteyy)

<u>YOU LEFT ME HALFWAY</u>

When walking in night,

You held my hand tight,

And promised me, you will be there by my side.

When sitting under the moon light,

You hugged me tight,

And promised me, you will be there in all my plights.

When lying under the stars,

You touched my scars,

And promised me, you will protect me from all the wars.

Not only my heart, you had also broken the promises you
made.

You left me alone halfway in a dark dreadful night with no
shade.

There's something about you I will always hate,

You made me wait and wait but didn't uphold the promises
you once made.

<u>DO THEY?</u>

Sometimes, I look in the mirror and don't recognize the eyes staring back at me.

I think of all the people roam around the cities that I have been to.

I try to make sense of every eye contact I made with the strangers around me.

Are they insecure too?

Do they also feel the same way I do?

It's okay, if no.

But if yes, don't worry I am stuck here too.

Just wave at me. And I will smile and wave back at you.

Beautifully Faded

Sonika Bhavta

(IG: @shonycaa)

<u>WOULD YOU BELIEVE</u>

Would you believe if I say

My heart skipped a beat

When it was about you

Maybe I never had enough for you.

Would you believe if I say

I always wanted to meet you halfway

At a point where both the

Earth and moon are equidistant.

Would you believe if I say

My silence is a voice

Sometimes it's the loudest one

That nobody could hear till day

But you...

Would you believe if I say

I fantasized fairy tales

Beautifully Faded

My idea of reality was skewed

leaving me all mused.

Would you believe if I say

I've always turned around every once

To rename the symphonies of your deception.

Would you believe if I say

You were my weakening eye

That never rose up to my horizon.

Would you believe if I say

Now I write my own sad songs

Our songs on the radio,

don't sound the same anymore...

Would you believe if I say

I gave up on the idea of love

I lost!

You were my idea of Love.

Soubhik Maji

(IG: @Soubhik_yaduvamshi)

<u>I DO STILL REMEMBER</u>

I do still remember the day when I hung between my parent's hand, crying and shaking myself as a protest against their wish.

I do still remember the day when everybody in the room sat alone as if we were from different planets.

I do still remember the days when we jumped to eat each other's tiffin leaving our own.

I do still remember the days when we went to fill our water bottles in a gang.

I do still remember the days when we in a gang went to the washroom for expressing our thoughts against the teachers.

I do still remember the days when we took a blazer to cover a guy and beat him without any reason.

I do still remember the days when our maths teacher would have been absent making it the best period of the day.

I do still remember the days when we used to kneel down in the corridors for not completing our homework.

I do still remember the days when a group of students used to get headache.

I do still remember the days when we used to do picnic in the last bench during the class.

I do still remember the days when our parents were called for our mischief.

Beautifully Faded

I do still remember the days when we used to get our result.

I do still remember the last day we were bound to leave the school, the treasure box of memories.

Srihari Rajagopalan

(IG: @srihari_r_nair)

<u>BEAUTIFULLY FADED</u>

All the trees and its leaves are green,

Its beauty cannot be admired if it's not seen.

You swirled into my life like a sparkling wine,

You threw away my pain all at a time.

You made me smile in my difficult phase,

All I had in my mind was your beautiful face.

You enlightened my life with your sweetened smile,

It could easily blow my mind a thousand mile.

My favorite place to rest my face was your palm,

That can easily take my pain and make me calm.

The more I knew you, the more I realized you were one of a kind,

Later I realized that I only had you in my mind.

Some days later I knew you started to walk far away,

But I knew it was late for me to find a way.

You came into my life like a striking thunder,

Later you made me think that I was a absolute blunder.

I fought midnights with my endless cries,

Then I realized how easily happiness flies.

Beautifully Faded

Your love for me was always an ecstasy,

After you left me I knew that you were just my fantasy.

Being a chef I had dealt always with cutlery's and
crockery's,

But now you made me dealt with a hurting memories.

A portrait will be really beautiful if it's well shaded,

At the end I witnessed as you beautifully faded.

Subhalaxmi Brahma

(IG: @i_am_suvu)

<u>THE FADED ESSENCE OF A FABLED BEAUTY</u>

She was born with a dream to grow,

But was unable to cope with the flow.

She just wanted to be independent,

But the wishes remained silent.

Deep down she determined to try again,

But with every try she got fallen.

She stood up to step forward,

But was forced to go backward.

Simply she adopted the situation,

Just to diminish the dream of creation.

Being abandoned was not so easy,

Just because she didn't want to be trendy.

She muted the echoes of heart,

Just to stay calm a little apart.

What would she do of the dreams got faded,

Just hugged the feelings of being regretted.

Somewhere dreams got bleached,

As the wings of dreams got clipped.

Beautifully Faded

The thunders accepted the charm,

With the transparent beauty of warm.

She chose the way of the essence be added,

With the colors of dreams that were being faded.

Broken heart was glued up with botox smiles,

As the dreams got tied up with broken kites.

Charming beauty got faded,

And she faded beautifully.

And she faded beautifully.

Sumit Garg

(IG: @Desi0810)

<ins>I FEEL I AM ALONE</ins>

I feel I am alone,
because I have wings but I cannot
fly.
I feel I am alone,
because I am happy but I cannot
smile.
I feel I am alone,
because I have light but there is
darkness in my life.
I feel I am alone,
because I have life but there is no life.
I feel I am alone,
because I have potential but I cannot
utilize.
I feel I am alone,
because I think I am alone.

<u>I FEEL FREE</u>

I feel free when,
I don't have to pretend what I am not.
I feel free when,
I fly in the sky being on the ground.
I feel free when,
There is darkness around me but I can
still see through it.
I feel free when,
I am surrounded by worries but have
smile on my face.
I feel free when,
I get stuck in the wind storm but
I know the way to pass through it.
I feel free when,
There is heavy downpour out but
have safe abode.
I feel free when,
There is flood out but I am
at the peak of mountain.
I feel free when,
I feel free.

Beautifully Faded

Surinder Bhardwaj

(IG: @bhardwajsurinder007)

LONE STANDING ALONE

I'm the lone standing tree

Playing in the lap of mother earth

Fed by the Sun and soil

Singing with the winds

Sometimes clouds come and shower their divine love on
me

Chatting with the birds

Few love to stay really long with me

A blissful lone standing tree.

<u>IT'S OKAY</u>

Its okay, not to be perfect,

God has created you unique in his own way,

Imperfection is just the mindset of judgmental people

You're simply perfect,

So, its okay, not to be perfect

Growth is the joy of life,

Curiosity of knowing is its salt,

Whatever you're,

Live it with your best,

As it's okay, not to be perfect

Rather achieving perfection,

Go for living the moment totally,

Live happily, give your best,

Rest everything forget

So relax, its okay,

Not to be perfect.

Suruchi Shiohare

(IG: @suruchi_shiohare08)

<u>LOVE</u>

It was you who made me feel

what actually love is…

Your touch made me feel,

Like stars are dancing around me.

Sitting next to you is like,

Taking a sip of stars,

sun, the whole universe.

And now,

You have made me feel like,

Every temporary thing feels like permanent,

For a reason.

I'll never fall away from the gift of us,

I want you beside me,

For the rest of my life.

Hold me in your arms,

Just like a small child.

If I could describe happiness in words,

I would write you.

Beautifully Faded

I found life,

In that moment,

When I found you.

Beautifully Faded

Swathi K Sorab

(IG: @swathikishansorab)

<u>THANK YOU TEACHER</u>

I was just a forbidden stone,

You sculpted me into a worthy idol.

I was aimless and confused,

You showed me a path to walk upon.

Darkness was all I knew, until one day,

When you lit up my life bright, you being my light.

Failure was always my weakness,

You taught me to step on it and try harder for success.

'Difficult' and 'Impossible' were something you never taught me,

'Determination' and 'Passion for success' are all I learnt from you.

You lit up the dark walls around me,

With the amazing shine of success.

I was a coward, I wanted to quit,

You became my strength all along.

My failure gave me only tears,

For you it was your failure too.

Yet you never gave up on me.

Beautifully Faded

Confidence was something I never lost with you by my
side,

You became the Foundation for my success.

You were the guide I needed all along,

The light I needed to look towards my goal.

You were my motivator, my Savior,

The only answer to all my questions.

You're someone I'd always look up to,

Along with books you taught me life too.

When for myself and the world I was nothing but a failure,

You taught me to shine in the glory of my success.

Words cannot be enough to describe the gratitude I have
for you, yet,

Thank you teacher, for making me what I'm today.

Beautifully Faded

Sweta Panda

(IG: @no_fault_in_my_stars)

<u>MY NIGHTMARES</u>

You are my nightmares

I exactly don't know what are your intentions

But you are always in my dreams

Only I can remember your pale face, luminous lips, and
glittering eyes

Your eyes have the power to allure me and make me stuck

I don't know what are your intentions

You look beautiful yet furious

There is an unknown fear when you look straight into my
eyes

Every night I ask you what your intentions are

But then you leave my hands

I felt like falling down

&

I wake up feeling helpless.

<u>I AM GETTING DRENCHED</u>

It's raining I am getting drenched

Completely drenched to fill in my thirst

The fear the anguish the darkness the thoughts

My mind and the anxiety of being happy and hiding my frown

I want to sing

I want to dance

I want to fly flaunting my wings high

I want to be carefree

But I m caged

Caged with the thoughts

Caged with the fear

Caged with the sorrows

The rope is tightly tied up in my feet

I want to move out

I want to scream

I want to live and feel alive

I want to rise above

I want to leap into ocean

I want to climb the mountains

I Am getting drenched with rain filling in my thirst.

Beautifully Faded

Tanisha Khunger

(IG: @ rh_ymetime_with_t.k)

<u>THE FROLIC SNOW</u>

Snowflakes bring joy,

It becomes in shape of every toy,

It seems very appraising but coy,

Snow eradicate the annoy.

"IT IS ALWAYS A WOW,"

"AS IT IS THE FROLIC SNOW."

Snow comes with little breeze,

But want to make everything freeze,

It creates the heart appease,

Snowflakes melts like cheese.

"IT MOVES IN A ASTONISHING ROW",

"AS IT'S THE FROLIC SNOW".

Beautifully Faded

THE UNDERWATER BLISS

Here life seems to be close
Actually it's full of gloss,

Many things are unbelievable
Still the sense is completely peasable,

The soul gets miss in THE UNDERWATER BLISS.

Every sound is amazing
Which makes your breath appraising,

The life here is fictitious
Still the thought is fabulous

The positive vibes feel like a kiss
In THE UNDERWATER BLISS.

The breeze over it take out every vail
And manifest you with your life's trail,

Each organism it include
Fascinate our mood,

Keep in mind never miss THE UNDERWATER BLISS.

Toyosi

(IG: @toyosioludare)
<u>HER WILL</u>

Dreams: a future aspiration, one she had but could not fulfil,

The will of her parents, stronger than hers, she didn't want to disappoint them,

She was tired, they didn't care, saying "we want the best for you"...

She pretended to be strong, in vain she fell, She wanted her life back, so courage she gathered,

Telling her parents wasn't easy, but she stood tall on her word, her parents succombed,

She has her life back, "it was worth it" she said.

<u>AND SHE FADED</u>

He wasn't there, she was his responsibility

All he had to do was protect her, but yet again, failure washed
over him like a tsunami...

The pain!, The guilt!, The regret!

The tears!, The hurt!, All he felt...

Now she lay there almost lifeless, but ever so beautiful

"Will she ever love me again?", He was doubtful...

"Please come back to me" he went saying

But her light was dim, she was fading.

Uma Deshpande

(IG: @umadeshpande3)

<u>DREAM</u>

I dream of the taste of your lips.

I dream of the smell of your cologne on my sheets.

I dream of getting lost in the depth of your eyes.

I dream of falling asleep to the lullaby of your heartbeats.

I dream of unraveling in your arms.

I dream of calling you mine.

<u>MY RELATIONSHIP STATUS</u>

My relationship status is 'in love'.

I am in love with the solitude that I disregarded when you were there. I didn't know it was so preaching.

I am in love with my resilience which you always undermined. I didn't know that it always comes from within.

I am in love with how comfortable I am in my own skin. I didn't know that molding myself according to your taste was gratuitous.

Did I really had to be crushed to fall in love with myself?

Now, when I look back to say 'I love you'

I find my reflection where you were there.

Beautifully Faded

Vanika Saberwal

(IG: @iamvanika)

<u>I CAN FEEL HER</u>

I could see her inside me,
She is ripped apart like me,
She is crying and screaming
But there is none to hear it.

The walls are so high around,
She wraps her in the corner of room,
Every sound makes her afraid,
Her body trembles like old and fade.

Loneliness is her best friend,
Compassion makes her vulnerable now,
She doesn't open her eyes anymore
As light makes her feel terrible more.

She is there, but she is not me,
She is real, but she is not me,
She cries in the pain,
But I fake the smile,
She screams in hurt,
I hug the silence,

I am not she; she is not me
But I feel her in me, she feels me outside.

Vritti Khapne

(IG: @perspicaciousthoughts)

<u>DARKNESS</u>

The dark night conjures as I lie on the bed, with eyes wide
open and the heart beats fasten,

There is silence all around me, but

Chaos in my mind

I try to move and suddenly feel a paralytic strike.

I struggle to think straight for once as I know,

If I don't, I'll be swallowed by the dark.

The ocean of tears, the hurricane of emotions, the lump in
my throat,

As I lie paralytic with dint of trust and hope.

The night goes by, the bright sun rises;

I crawl out of the bed with nothing but a smile on my face.

I hope they could see the darkness in me,

And save me from drowning in it.

For I don't blame them, because it's the trust that lacks,

And it was the only thing that leads me to a dark side.

<u>LOVE</u>

Love me until the ocean's dry,

Hold me as the clouds passes by.

For this love is not just between you and me but between
our souls;

Magnifying what we feel.

A lover's love, a mother's love,

The love when the clouds entangles with the mountain's
peak,

And unknowingly with the ocean's deep.

Love, a single word yet with so many meanings.

For few it's happy, for few sad, for few tormenting or
maybe a dark side.

So just take a deep breath and let the wind slide over your
cheeks,

Let fresh grass tickle your feet and look at the sky above
with the moon at its brightest and stars besides,

For its love what actually feels like if you never felt before.

As time passes everything fades, but love remains.

So love everything around and every feeling you feel as it
gives us a chance to dive in its epiphany.

Yogita Wagh

(IG: @yogitaonline2002)

<u>IN SEARCH OF</u>

In search of triumph, destined to the path of living alone

In search of serenity, destined to the path of living alone

In search of perfection, destined to the path of living alone

In search of positive self image, destined to the path of living alone

In search of being indifferent, destined to the path of living alone

In search of delight, destined to the path of living alone

In search of oneself, destined to the path of living alone

In search of musings verbatim, destined to the path of living alone

In search of morals, destined to the path of living alone

In search of nowhere, destined to the path of living alone.

<u>BEFORE YOU</u>

Before you speak, think.

Before you hate, forgive.

Before you lose, Hope.

Before you love, understand.

Before you cry, Smile.

Before you get, give.

Before you go, live.

Before you sleep, Dream

Before you fear, Trust.

Before you regret Take lessons.

Before you limit yourself, Unleash.

Before you forget, Acquire.

Before you write, Verbetise.

Beautifully Faded

Zainab Mazhar Kagalwala

(IG: @murmurinmind)

<u>GREATEST STRENGTH</u>

Greatest strength..

When I was shattered..

No one by my side...

Situations erupted..

No one knew I was right.....

Was all alone..

The whole day..

And the whole night...

At this time..there was this tiny hand..

Holding me tight..

Yes.. My daughter..

Who was always by my side..

Smiling and forcing me to live right..

Have gained my strength from this little angel..

Whose magic wand shone bright..

Somewhere She knew..

She knew..

She knew.. She had to throw the light...

On the path ahead..

Beautifully Faded

To get things back to life...

Little did I know..

My daughters grew so beautifully..

To hold their Mother and free her from fright...

Cant be enough Thankful to God..

To give me my Daughters

And make them my Pride!

Today we hold each others hand..

And walk through the roads…

And yes we are

Alright!!!!!